A Cricketing Dream

A Cricketing Dream

CHRIS MAY

Copyright © 2012 by CHRIS MAY.

ISBN: Softcover   978-1-4797-1498-8
               Ebook   978-1-4797-1499-5

This is a work of fiction. Names, characters, places and incidents either are the product of the author's imagination or are used fictitiously, and any resemblance to any actual persons, living or dead, events, or locales is entirely coincidental.

This book was printed in the United States of America.

To order additional copies of this book, contact:
Xlibris Corporation
0-800-644-6988
www.Xlibrispublishing.co.uk
Orders@Xlibrispublishing.co.uk
305000

Contents

FOR MR. M AND THE TWO MRS. M'S.
I OWE YOU EVERYTHING.

1

The Dream

"Matthew!!" shouted Mr. Temple, as thousands of cheering fans streamed from the London Cricket Ground one sunny Saturday in May. 13 year old Matthew Temple, or 'Matty' as he was known to his friends, sat staring aimlessly into the clear evening sky. He was daydreaming. Minutes ago, England had just thumped Australia once again to win the Champions Cup, and Jimmy Appleton had once again been England's match-winner. Appleton was the world's greatest batsman and had just broken the World Record for the number of sixes hit in a Champions Cup game.

'I wish *I* could play cricket like Jimmy Appleton', whispered Matty to himself, as he stared into the distance. Matty saw *himself* smashing 6 after 6 after 6 to help *his* team win the cup.

The trouble was, Matty, although desperate to, didn't play cricket as he wasn't very good at *anything*. Football, rugby, tennis, you name it he was hopeless. This was a problem for him, especially during PE lessons at school. Matty hated PE. Whichever sport was being played, Matty was simply terrible at it.

"Matthew, come on son, we are going to miss our train home!!" shouted Dad.

'*Cricket* will be the same' he whispered to himself, as he finally got up to make his way home with Dad. Dad himself, had been a fantastic cricketer in his time and would often tell Matty of his time in the game.

The train journey home was fantastic, as hundreds of England's army of supporters sang songs in celebration of their great win. Matty joined in and had great fun while his dad sat back and relaxed.

As Matty lay in bed that evening, with the thoughts of a fantastic day's cricket and the swashbuckling, daredevil deeds of Jimmy Appleton still clear in his mind, Matty kept repeating: "I wish I could play like Jimmy, I *wish* I could play like Jimmy . . . . But cricket will be the same".

But this time, for once, he said to himself: "I *will* do it, I *will* try cricket!"

And with that thought in his head, Matty drifted off to sleep, dreaming once again of one day being *his* team's match-winner.

2 ◣

Will He? Won't He?

S outhlands Cricket Club had been dad's club.

25 years ago, Trevor Temple was the best player at Southlands. He was the best player in the local County Senior league. He broke record after record as he destroyed the opposition bowlers week upon week and was given the nickname 'Typhoon'.

Matty never saw his Dad play cricket. A serious knee injury had ended his career before Matty was born. The injury occurred while he was batting for Southlands in a league match. While running between the wickets, the spikes on the sole of his left boot got caught in the grass and made his knee twist badly. Despite months of treatment and an operation, he didn't recover and never played again.

Dad could never bring himself to go back to Southlands. It was too upsetting for him not being able to play. He still watched the game on television as much as he possibly could, but never at his old club or at any other local ground.

Matty's Mum Lisa was a former catering assistant at Woods Hall, Southlands' home ground. That's how she met Matty's Dad. *Her* time there ended at the same time as his – it just wasn't the same without 'Typhoon' being there.

Lisa was a really friendly, gentle soul, who looked after her 'boys' with undying love. She really spoiled them. If cricket was on television, Matty and his dad would watch it excitedly while Mum would prepare lunches and teas just like she did at Woods Hall, with huge sandwiches and gorgeous sponge cakes laced with lashings of jam and cream. Matty particularly loved her chocolate sponges – his face covered in chocolate every time he devoured slice after slice of Mum's scrumptious cake!

Mum, like Dad, was keen for Matty to try his luck at cricket, but was the sort of person who, also like Dad, preferred not to push him too hard. "Matthew, get yourself down to the ground son," she would often say, but after mentioning it to him once, she wouldn't repeat herself, preferring to wait a while before trying again

Dad always told him each Sunday morning – despite his own wish never to go back – to go to Woods Hall and 'Learn to play the greatest game in the World' instead of 'Wasting time on video games and computers', or 'Mucking about at Felton Field'.

"I'm *going* to Southlands" Matty said to himself as he awoke the morning after England's great win.

Sundays were junior training days and many of Matty's classmates from school would make their way to Woods Hall every week, in the hope that one day, they too, could play like the legendary 'Typhoon', this mythical figure from years gone by – never knowing he was in fact, Matty's Dad.

"Mum, Dad, I'm off to meet Johnny", shouted Matty as he hurriedly finished his toast and scampered out of the front door, down the street.

Johnny Harris was Matty's best friend and he, like Matty was not very good at sport, so together, they shared their woes. They would meet at Johnny's every Sunday morning and either play on video games or watch DVD's in Johnny's bedroom.

Only, this week he wasn't off to meet Johnny.

Matty skipped his way along Herald Street, down Ropers Lane, across Felton Field and onto Dean Terrace, where, halfway along stood Woods Hall. Once there, he could not bring himself to make his way through the car park toward the clubhouse. Every time he took a faltering step forward, his brain kept telling him to take another one back. After what seemed like an eternity, but in reality was only 20 minutes, Matty ran for his life through the car park and through the double doors into the Southlands clubhouse. In the reception area, photos of old players and teams filled the walls, and there, the biggest one of all, sat proudly below the club badge. It was a black and white photograph of Matty's Dad, standing proudly with the County Senior League trophy. Beneath the photo, a white card with black ink simply said: 'The Typhoon, Southlands' Player of the Century'.

"WOWW" exclaimed Matty, totally in awe of his Father's achievements, his Dad having never told him *this* much about his career.

The Woods Hall ground was over 150 years old. The current clubhouse was relatively new, but the player's pavilion to the left, was nearly 100 years old. It was truly, a magnificent building, with the changing rooms on the first floor, which then had balconies overlooking the playing area for the players to watch their games. The ground floor seating area was for members only. Most of the ground was beautifully tree lined, and on the far side standing proudly above the trees, was the spire of Southlands Cathedral. It really was a gorgeous sight, and every local player always looked forward to playing against Southlands, just so they could always say they had played at the historic Woods Hall. The playing area was beautifully mown and was looked after by head groundsman Jim Wakefield.

When he had calmed himself down, Matty made his way to the rear of the reception, where the doors which opened out onto the field were ajar. He could hear the appeals of the bowlers and cries of "Shottt" from loads of boys and girls who were scampering around the lush green outfield, enjoying every minute of their Sunday morning's cricket. He recognised Adam Elliott and Luke Anderson from school, and he knew Connor Bennett, who lived around the corner from him. But Matty just could not take the next steps out onto hallowed turf.

'They will just laugh at me', he thought as he struggled with his emotions. From there, he darted back through the reception, back through the car park, along Dean Terrace and all the way back to Johnny's to carry on with a 'normal' Sunday.

"I will do it next week", he muttered to himself as he approached Johnny's front door.

Next Sunday came and went, as did the following Sunday, and the next, and still Matty, despite making his way to the ground, simply *could* not take those steps onto the Woods Hall field, each time venturing back to Johnny's house until finally, one July morning, the steps were more or less taken for him.

"Hello young man, can we help you?" said a voice from somewhere. Matty looked around and there, stood at the opposite end of the reception, was a tall figure with a bald head, except for a band of brown hair at the back, thick moustache, and he was wearing a pair of silly looking half mast trousers.

"Err . . . err . . . . I-I've c-c-come to watch the cricket," stuttered Matty.

"Well, you have come to the right place then son," said the man. The man's name was Bill Simpson, and little did Matty know, how much this conversation would change his life . . .

PLAYER PROFILE

Full name Trevor Temple

Nickname Typhoon

Born September 15, 1961,

Major teams Southlands CC

Batting style Right-hand bat

Club Appearances 147

Runs 6489 at an average of 48.67

Highest Score: 209 n.o. versus Hurworth, August 1984

Honours County Senior League leading run scorer: 1982, 83, 84, 85, 86, 87. National Cup winner 1985.

Dream Fact His 209 versus Hurworth was scored off only 131 balls!

Best Known For Smashing opposition bowling attacks apart. His record of 46 sixes hit in a season in 1984 is still a County Senior League record.

Do mention County League batting records

Do not mention The knee injury sustained while batting against Rockliffe in 1988, which ended his career at the age of only 26.

3

Simple Cricket

Bill Simpson – or 'Simple' as he was known to everyone at Woods Hall, was an old team mate of 'Typhoon' Temple. They played together in the 1984 County Senior League Championship side as well as the 1983 County Senior League Cup and the 1985 National Cup winning teams.

'Simple' was a wily old fox who bowled little medium paced deliveries which batsmen could never seem to get away. Supporters used to say: "If Wimpy cannot get you with the ball, Typhoon will get you with his bat!"

He was also a very strange looking man, with a band of thick brown hair around the back of his head, which would stick out at the sides, a thick brown moustache and he had what seemed like a permanent grin on his face, revealing huge white teeth! It looked like bolts of electricity were causing his hair to stand on end. He basically resembled a wild sweeping brush!! With that and the limp with which he walked, he really was a sight to behold! He also had this funny habit of repeating himself over and over again, and he had a strange accent at times, saying words like "Booling" instead of bowling and "Feeelding" instead of fielding.

Now in his fifties, Simple looked after the junior coaching at Southlands every Sunday morning. Sometimes, up to 40 youngsters would be there, waiting for their instructions off him.

Now, a new face had arrived at the Simpson cricketing school.

"You've come to watch have you son?" asked Simple with interest.

"Y-y-y-yes" replied Matty nervously.

"What's your name son? Do you not want to have a game?" said Simple.

"My n-name's Matthew. I-I-I don't think so, I th-think I will j-just w-watch," spluttered Matty.

"OK Matthew, come outside then," said Simple.

So, very nervously, Matty followed Simple out onto the field, trying to hide behind him as he did so. But it did not work.

"Whey hey, it's Matty," shouted a voice. It belonged to Danny Davison. Danny was in the same Year 9 class at Hartson School. He was the class clown, always telling jokes, poking fun at other people's misfortune and was generally a nuisance.

"What's Useless doing here?" he continued loudly.

"Hey, less of that Mr Davison thank you," replied Simple. "This lad has just come down to watch, so keep your comments to yourself.

"That's a good job then Mr Simpson, because he is rubbish at everything!" said Danny.

"OK, well we will see about that Danny lad," said Simple.

Matty then spent the next hour watching the kids go through their practice routines and have a game to finish off the session. He sent Johnny a text message from his mobile phone, telling him he was going to be late arriving at his house – not telling him the real reason why – for now at least.

After the session was over, Simple limped over to Matty to ask him if he would be coming again the following Sunday.

"I think so," whispered Matty.

"Good lad," replied Simple. "Maybe next week you will join in eh?" he said quizzically.

Just then, the boys he knew, such as Luke Anderson, Harry Bennett and Mark Elliott came over.

"Are you going to try and play cricket Matty?" asked Harry.

"Don't know", replied Matty quietly.

"Mr Simpson, it will take more than just Sunday morning practice to make him into a cricketer!" Luke exclaimed cruelly.

"Leave him alone," shouted Mark Elliott.

With that, Matty quickly left the club and ran to Johnny's, keen to keep his morning's news to himself. Johnny asked him what had made him late.

"Been doing jobs with Dad" was all he could think of quickly enough in response. Johnny knew that Matty wasn't telling the truth, but left it at that, so their usual Sunday morning continued.

At school the next day, Matty was faced with a lot of cruel taunts and comments about his lack of sporting ability from the boys who had seen him at Southlands the previous morning.

"Useless, Useless" cried Danny Davison.

Johnny, wondering why the taunts were all aimed at Matty instead of them both, asked him.

"Don't know," replied Matty

"Hey, Johnny, are you gonna to join Useless at cricket next Sunday then? You can be the Useless Brothers! Ha, ha, ha,ha,haaaaa!!" shouted Luke Anderson

Johnny now knew where Matty had been and why he was late.

"*Why* couldn't you tell me the truth mate?" asked Johnny. "We tell each other *everything*. You *know* you can trust me".

"I didn't want anyone to know mate" he replied. "I just really want to get into cricket, but being so bad at everything else, I would hate to let Dad down at the game he loves. I really wanted to tell you but thought that once I had been, tried the game out, been bad at it and left, I would then just carry on as if it had never happened."

"Look mate," said Johnny, "I'll go with you next Sunday and just watch. You join in and see if you like it"

"Would you?" exclaimed Matty, 'That would be fantastic!"

"Of course mate, no problem," replied Johnny.

The following Sunday came round quickly, and Matty met Johnny outside Woods Hall just as the practice session started, so that they didn't catch any of the other children on there way in, thus risking the chance of Danny and the rest poking fun at them. They went into the reception where Matty proudly showed Johnny the photo of his Dad, still taking pride of place on the honours board.

"Gosh!!" cried an amazed Johnny. "Is that *really* your Dad?? That's fantastic! Why has he never mentioned anything about this?"

"I think it hurts him he cannot play anymore mate," replied Matty.

The two boys made their way onto the field. Johnny continued to the seating area next where the practice sessions took place, while Matty lingered around with the others, who were waiting for Wimpy to arrive.

Upon his arrival, Wimpy quickly introduced Matty to the others. One or two – the usual suspects – sniggered as Simple told them all Matty's name.

"His name is Useless, not Matthew," bellowed Danny Davison.

"That is enough Mr Davison, I warned you last week!" replied Simple sternly.

Once Simple had got the children to lap the outfield to warm up, he asked Matty to stay with him. He re-assured him that this was not a competition and that, as long as Matty enjoyed his cricket, that was the main thing. But for Matty, enjoyment alone wasn't enough. Having seen his Dad's glorious photo in the clubhouse, he desperately wanted to be good – just at this one thing.

As the fielding drills began, it quickly became obvious that being good at cricket would take some seriously hard work. Every time the ball was thrown to him, either in the air or along the ground, he either fumbled it or dropped it.

"Ha ha, Useless!!" came the cries as Matty stumbled from one mistake to another. Wimpy did not like this at all, so called everyone in for a serious talk.

"Look, we are here to enjoy our cricket, not poke fun at people. Keep your comments to yourself or go home," bellowed Simple.

It got worse for Matty as the practice games began. Every time a bowler sent a delivery down to him when he batted, he simply just could not hit the ball. Tears began to trickle from his eyes as the feeling of utter despair and helplessness quickly came over him.

As the session drew to a close, Simple pulled Matty to one side and repeated his earlier comments about the sessions not being competitions.

"Don't worry son," said Simple. "Cricketers are not made in a day you know. 'Keep coming every week and you *will* get better.'"

"I'll help you Matty," said a quiet voice from behind Simple.

It was Sophie Jameson, one of the several girls who took part every Sunday. Sophie was a very good cricketer, who played for the County under 15s. "If you want to, we can stay behind every Sunday and I will practice with you," she continued.

"Would you do that for *me*?" asked Matty. "Really?? Wow, that would be great. Thanks!" he said.

So for the next couple of Sundays, after each of Simple's sessions, Sophie would practice with Matty on every aspect of his game, while Johnny watched on, making sure his best mate was OK. Progress was slow. Matty just did not have any co-ordination and his performance was poor.

"Come down to some matches on a Saturday and play in the games we have at the bottom of the ground and get to know some of the guys in the teams Matty," said Sophie one morning. "You'll have a great time. You come too Johnny," she added.

The next part of Matty's education was about to begin . . .

PLAYER PROFILE

Full name William Granville (Bill) Simpson

Nickname Simple

Born September 15, 1953,

Major teams Southlands CC

Batting style Right-hand bat

Bowling style Right-arm medium

Club Appearances 408

Wickets 1136

Best Bowling 8 for 11 versus Marston, June 1979

Honours County Senior League leading wicket taker: 1975, 78, 79, 80, 81. National Cup winner 1985.

Dream Fact He once took hat-tricks in 2 consecutive matches.

Best Known For Bizarre outbursts like "Buzzy buzzy bees", "Tea anyone", "God makes the rain" and "Never get there, it'll never get there"

4

Match Day At Woods Hall

Match days at Woods Hall were great occasions. Hundreds of local people would flock to see the Southlands team pit their wits against the best sides in local cricket, in the County Senior League. Modern day stars were captain Tony Fisher, opening batsman James Hilton, middle order hitman Chris Marshall and fiery fast bowler Robbie White. These guys were massively popular players and week after week, they would provide marvellous entertainment for the crowds.

On the last Saturday in July, Southlands were at home to neighbours Marston, and the ground was packed. Matty and Johnny made their way in and met Sophie and her mates who were having one of their usual games down in the far corner of the ground. They were quickly made to feel welcome and even Johnny joined in. No-one questioned their ability and despite them being far worse that the others, both lads had a great time.

Simple was down at the ground, and today was the first time Matty heard one of his legendary quotes. He had this annoying habit of repeating himself time and again, much to the annoyance of the club members.
Every matchday, Simple would make his way around the ground, asking spectators whether or not they would like to buy their tea, which they could enjoy in the clubhouse while the teams had theirs.

"Tea anyone? Anybody want a tea, tea? Tea? Anyone want tea?," he would say as he lapped the field. By the time he reached Matty and the gang, he completed his lap. "Any of you lot want a tea? Tea?

"No thanks Bill" came the collective reply, and as he began to make his may to the clubhouse to tell the tea ladies how many had been bought, he let out a huge long cry of "TEEEEEEEEEEA!!" Matty and the others were creased up laughing, while Simple was oblivious to it all!

Matty and Johnny had a great time and couldn't wait for the next day's practice session. Sadly, it was not to be like the previous day, as Matty, while Johnny watched as always, continued where he left off the previous Sunday, with mistake after mistake, even falling over when he spilled one attempted catch. Once again, the awful taunts came, and once again, Simple and Sophie would re-assure Matty and urge him to keep going. Sophie also told him to keep going to the ground on Saturdays to play in the games at the bottom corner and to not listen to the horrible boys.

'Just *enjoy* your cricket Matty', Sophie would always say.

The next couple of Saturdays came and went and Matty, very slowly showed some signs of improvement and this translated into improvement at the Sunday practices. He was by no means good, but at least took some catches and stopped balls going to the boundary instead of allowing them to go through his legs. His batting improved too. Although he hadn't yet mastered any attacking shots, he could at least play defensive ones, which Wimpy wanted everyone to have the ability to play.

All the while, as Matty and Johnny made their visits to Woods Hall, their parents were unaware of them, both of them informing that on Saturdays they were simply on Felton Field playing with the lads, and on Sundays they were at each other's houses.

As Matty improved, Simple in fact, picked him for an under 15 match away at Seaton Park, as several players were away playing for the county, and told Matty he could travel to the game in his car. Matty had to make more excuses so his Mum and Dad didn't find out he was playing cricket.

Two months ago, Matty couldn't catch a ball to save his life. Now he was in a Southlands team, just like his Dad. It couldn't get much better than this could it?

The trip to Seaton Park was the next leg of Matty's cricket journey.

5

Away Days

Simple had an old silver car which really needed to be replaced. There was rust all over it, and inside, the carpets were scruffy and worn. The inside of the roof was covered by dirty felt, except for a circular piece, immediately above where the driver's head would be. His head must have worn the felt away. It was so smooth and shiny it looked like a mirror!!

"Come on lads", said Simple, as the team assembled in the club car park. "Time to go. Matthew, you can come in my car."

As well as Simple, Sophie's Mum had her car and the other car taking players to Seaton belonged to Alan Moxon, whose nickname was 'Coach'. 'Coach' Moxon was the first team manager, and had played for Southlands in the 1960s. He was a magnificent fast bowler in his time and had even played 2 test matches for England. He was a grumpy old soul who had no time for players who lacked effort and passion. He always spoke his mind, and would often tell players how bad they were, especially if they didn't try hard enough. One second team off spinner in particular, would often get the sharp end of Moxon's tongue:

"Dave McConnell, you are certainly, the WORST spin bowler I have ever seen in my life. Don't waste my time and everyone else's by turning up here lad!" Moxon would often scream at the unfortunate McConnell

On the way down to the game, Simple came out with another of his famous repetitions, as a massive bee flew into the car through an open window. The Matty and the other players in the back of the car squirmed and squealed in fear of being stung. The bee quickly flew away, but not before Simple kept saying:

"Buzzy buzzy bees, buzzy bees. You don't need to be frightened of a buzzy bee!! Buzzy buzzy bees .... Bees .... Buzzy bees."

The boys then had to hold their laughs in so as not to embarrass Simple!

They arrived at Seaton Park and Simple introduced Matty to coach Moxon. In order to stop people from realising who Matty was, he told Wimpy his surname was Thompson. The mearest mention of the name Temple would surely have made alarm bells ring in Simple and coach Moxon's heads.

The team warmed up on the outfield and Matty seemed to do himself justice, not dropping many catches, so he was in good spirits as the players went back to the dressing room for a final pre-match team talk.

Sadly, rain started falling heavily, and after half an hour, the team managers decided to call the match off. A huge groan echoed around the changing room when Simple told his players the news. Cue another Simple moment:

"God makes the rain, don't blame me for the rain . . . . Don't blame me for the rain, God makes the rain!" Simple exclaimed which brought yet more giggles from the players.

Matty was chosen for another game the following week in which, although he didn't score any runs, he gave his all in the field, which pleased Wimpy and coach Moxon.

As the days and weeks went by, Matty really got himself and Johnny involved at Southlands, helping with scoring and providing the interval drinks for the players, and generally they just enjoyed being around the place, as Sophie and the gang continued to make them feel really welcome. Sundays weren't as bad either, as the improvements Matty made, ensured the number of horrible comments from the like of Danny Davison were made less frequently.

Coach Moxon *really* liked the way in which Matty began to put everything into his cricket on and off the field and started to rely on him more and more.

"Son, you keep doing what you're doing and you will be just fine. Never mind what the idiots say on a Sunday, keep practising and one day you'll make a really good club cricketer", Moxon told Matty one Saturday.

He asked Matty to do the scorebook for the first team in their National Cup semi final at home to Great Foxton as the usual scorer was on holiday, which Matty simply could not believe. He jumped at the chance, and could not wait to witness the exploits of the likes of Hilton, Marshall and White.

This was Southlands' first *real* crack at the National Cup since they won the competition in 1985, when 'Simple' and 'Typhoon' were in their pomp. It had become something of a 'Holy Grail' for everyone associated with the Woods Hall club, particularly captain Tony Fisher, who was an 11 year old boy when Southlands were National champions in 1985. He was desperate to emulate his heroes and bring the National Cup back to Woods Hall.

After Typhoon's career ended, and Simple's retirement, Southlands had suffered a loss of form, with many of the other stars of the 1980s also reaching the end of their careers. The 1990s were a barren time for Southlands, with 6th being their highest league position way back in 1991. They then suffered the humiliation of being relegated to the County League Division 2 in 1994. With that, crowd numbers dropped, sponsorship was lost and the club were in serious trouble.

After a couple of years of struggle, the committee decided something had to be done. Wimpy was made junior development manager, coach Moxon was brought back to the club, and Tony Fisher was made first team captain. Over the next few years, with Moxon at the helm, Fisher leading from the front on the field and Simple bringing through a host of junior talent, Southlands made gentle progress up division 2, eventually winning it in 2002, bringing Senior League cricket back to Woods Hall.

By 2008, with the younger players like Hilton, Marshall, White and Peter Stephenson gaining in confidence more progress was made and once again, Southlands had become a force to be reckoned with. The last three seasons had seen them take the runners up spot in the County Senior League, which guaranteed a place in the coveted National competition.

Southlands dominated the second half of their semi final and won by 7 wickets, after a blistering 80 ball century from James Hilton and a 48 ball half century from Chris Marshall. Robbie White had earlier taken 4 wickets as Great Foxton had looked like setting a target which may have been out of Southlands' reach. As it was, White's late burst of wickets kept the Foxton total down to 283 from their 50 overs.

After the game, Coach Moxon thanked Matty for doing a fantastic job, and told him he would be first reserve for the scorer's job for the final.

What Matty didn't realise, was that this year's final would be at the London Cricket Ground, scene of Jimmy Appleton's destruction of Australia. When Moxon told him, he almost fell to the floor!!

"Whatever happens son, make sure you are on the bus with *us* for the final. If you're not scoring, we'll need all the support we can get in the ground, whoever we play", said Moxon.

Their opponents would be Elton Cricket Club, current National champions and winners of the competition in 3 of the last 4 years. They were also the current Super League champions. The Super League is a competition, only for National champions. Teams from England, Australia, New Zealand, South Africa, Pakistan and India battle it out over 2 weeks to decide the winner.

It was going to be a huge task to wrestle the trophy from the all-powerful Londoners, whose ground was less than 2 miles from the LCG. This final was more like a home game for the men from Central Road.

To be safe, Matty and Johnny decided to tell their parents some of the truth – that they had been going to Southlands for the last few Saturdays watching cricket and that the following Saturday, they would be travelling on the team bus to the LCG. When Matty told his Dad, he was amazed,

'Good lad Matthew son, but why didn't you tell me?!', said Dad excitedly. "I *told* you cricket was well worth trying. 'Mum will make sure you get on the bus OK and pick you up from the club when you get back. I will watch the game on TV".

Mum was thrilled: 'Oh Matthew that is fantastic! I told you, you would enjoy it. I'll get you there on the morning and be there for you when you get back to the ground in the evening'.

Cricket fever swept Southlands as preparations were made for the trip to London. Flags, banners and rosettes were made for supporters to take with them. Ten coaches were booked to take hundreds of them on the 200 mile journey to the Capital. Even local newspaper and radio reporters got involved, interviewing the players, asking them how they believed they would do and what they felt it would take to defeat the mighty Londoners.

The three weeks between the semi and grand final went by in a flash and the night before the game, Matty simply could not sleep as his mind raced with dreams of the Southlands lads taking the cup back to Woods Hall for the first time in almost 30 years

PLAYER PROFILE

Full name Alan Davis Moxon

Nickname Coach

Age 72,

Major teams Southlands CC, Yorkshire, England

Batting style Right-hand bat

Bowling Style Right arm fast

Club Appearances 102

Wickets 583 at an average of 11.01

Best Bowling: 9 for 21 for Yorkshire versus Hampshire, May 1962

Honours 2 test appearances for England. County Senior League leading wicket taker 1967,68,69.

Dream Fact His 9 wickets against Hampshire came from only 11 overs bowled!

Best Known For Playing for England

Do mention Alan Moxon

Do not mention Lazy cricketers. Dave McConnell

Cricket Bits and Pieces

For readers with little or no cricket knowledge, here are a few bits of information to describe terms you will see in the remainder of the book, which should help your understanding of them.

Pitch

22 yards in length, it is the piece of ground prepared in the middle of the field where the bowler bowls at the batsman.

Over

Group of 6 balls bowled by a bowler to the facing batsman.

Delivery

Another term for a ball bowled by the bowler.

Stumps/Wickets

Set of poles (usually wooden) with two wooden bails on the top, which the bowler aims for when bowling at the batsman. These are situated at each end of the pitch.

On/Off Strike

The batsman on strike is the one facing the bowling. The batsman off strike stands at the bowler's end of the pitch.

Crease

The area marked by white lines where the batsman stands and bowlers bowl from.

Dismissals

When a batsman is out, he is dismissed, and can be dismissed by being:

Bowled (ball hits the stumps)

Caught (including off the gloves as well as the bat),

Leg Before Wicket (LBW – Ball hits the batsman's padded leg before the bat and would have gone on to hit the stumps).

Run out (batsman hits the ball, attempts to run to the other end of the pitch, and a fielder hits the stumps with the ball before the batsman reaches the other end).

Stumped (Similar to a run out, but this time, the wicketkeeper does the work when the batsman misses the ball and leaves his batting crease.

CRICKET FIELDING POSITIONS

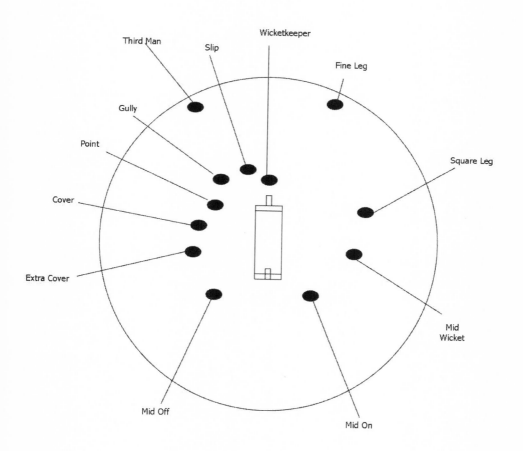

6

The Final (Part 1) Catastrophe!!

The day of the final was finally here. A first class coach was arranged to take the 12 man Southlands squad and backroom team – including Matty, and his best mate of course – to the LCG in style, while the rest of the convoy followed behind. Matty and Johnny sat excitedly together as Matty told his tales of his previous visit to the famous old stadium. When they arrived, the passengers in the first coach were ushered into the pavilion while supporters were taken to the North Stand. The old pavilion was an awe inspiring place, full of photographs, trophies and souvenirs of bygone years. The group gave a collective "WOHH!" as they made their way around the place. The players were taken up into the away dressing room, while the dozen or so others went into the London Cricket Club members room for pre-match refreshments.

It was almost a home game for Elton, and the LCG was rapidly filling up with home support.

As the day progressed, the players from both sides began their routines on the lush, immaculate outfield, which basically resembled a stripy green carpet. Everything went smoothly until 5 minutes before the end of the warm up session, disaster struck!

As the Southlands players went through their final catching routine, Chris Marshall and Mike Cullen both went for the same ball instead of one of them calling their name assertively.

BANG!!!

The two of them collided and collapsed to the ground in a heap. The rest of the squad rushed over to them to see how they were. They were in a mess. They had clashed heads and both of them had suffered terrible cuts. Both needed hospital treatment. What were Southlands going to do? They only had one substitute with them. That would still leave them with only 10 players. They couldn't go into a National final with just 10! Coach Moxon frantically went up to the members area to see if there were any players among the group of supporters. There were none. They were all too old, the second team were on their way to their own cup final in Wales the following day. There just wasn't anyone . . .

"Matthew is here," came a voice. It was Simple's.

"Matthew can play," he said.

"Matthew???" said Moxon, amazed Matty's name had even been mentioned.

"Look Alan," said Simple. "Matthew will give his all on that field. He may not be the best player in the world, but he will give everything for you out there today."

"Yes!" "Give him a game!" Give him a go!" came voices around the members room.

"But he's too young, too small, he has no kit with him, he hasn't played senior cricket before, he can't hit the ball, he can hardly catch the ball. He is a lovely lad and I like him a lot, but it is not fair on *him*," muttered Moxon forcefully.

"Alan, he can borrow kit from one of the injured lads, he could roll the sleeves and trouser legs up, and just wear his trainers to play in. "It is better than just having ten men!" urged Simple

After a few seconds, coach Moxon relented and said, "OK, if he is *all* we have he will have to do!"

While all of this was going on, Matty stood in the background, amazed Simple had even mentioned his name! As coach Moxon agreed to allow him to play, Matty suddenly shook in a mixture of fear and excitement, his heart thumping inside his chest so hard, he thought his chest would burst! Moxon grabbed him and led him quickly down the stairs into the dressing room area. As he did so, Matty felt compelled to tell everyone his secret. "My real name is Matthew Temple!!" he exclaimed.

Moxon stopped. "Temple?" he asked. "You are not Trevor's lad are you??" he asked.

"Y – yes" Matty replied.

"Bill, Bill, Matthew is Typhoon's lad" shouted Moxon from the stairs.

"Eh??" Simple responded. "Well if he is anything like his Dad, he'll be fine out there today. The big games were always the best for Typhoon. 'Get him ready and on that field!!"

The players frenziedly cut up Chris Marshall's whites so they would at least fit somewhere approaching properly and captain Fisher sprinted out onto the field to give the umpires the team sheet in time to toss up with Elton captain Rob Pickering.

At the toss, the LCG hummed with expectation. Television reporters and cameras swarmed around the captains. The atmosphere was electric! Pickering spun the coin and Fisher called heads. It was a tail. Pickering immediately elected to bat, thinking that *any* score his side made would be enough against a depleted Southlands batting line up.

Once back in the Southlands dressing room, the skipper gave a pre match team talk, welcoming the substitutes, Matty and Paul Vose and urging his players to give everything they had, "We know Matty and Paul will give it their all today. Lads, we shall win this for 'Cull' and Chris, come on!" exclaimed Fisher firmly.

The bell to signal the umpire's entrance onto the field rang, and a huge roar of expectation and excitement erupted around the packed stadium. Fisher then led his side out to silence, bar a few shouts of encouragement from the 500 or so visitors from Southlands, who had made the journey south. As the Elton opening batsmen Pickering and Joe McShane made their way down the pavilion steps, huge waves of sound echoed around the LCG as the Elton supporters urged their men on.

Captain Fisher gave the new ball to Robbie White and Kyle Donovan. Fisher set his fielding positions carefully, placing Matty at fine leg – away from the high pressure positions (or so he thought).

Bowling from the Pavilion End of the ground, White sprinted in at full throttle and bowled like the wind, his first 3 balls missing the outside edge of Pickering's bat by a whisker. Pickering took a quick single off the fourth ball, eager to get off strike. McShane looked nervous as he took guard and awaited White's next delivery. It was a beauty. It came at McShane at searing pace, thudding heavily into his front pad. 'HOWZAAAATTT!!!!' came the cry from the whole Southlands team. The umpire's finger was up. McShane was out leg before wicket first ball!!!

Kyle Donovan bowled the second over from the Media Centre End of the ground, at Pickering. He couldn't lay a bat on any of Donovan's missile-like deliveries.

In the next over, White continued his spell. The first two balls were blocked by Dan Farnham, struggling with White's pace and bounce.

The third was slightly off target, allowing Farnham to pull towards the mid wicket boundary, the ball pulling up just short, enabling him to run three. Pickering was back on strike, fidgeting nervously at the crease. White steamed in and WHACK!! Pickering's middle stump was sent cartwheeling down towards the Media Centre! Elton were now 4 for 2!

Elton's star batsman Aidan Healey made his way to the crease in virtual silence. The opening salvo from the Southlands men had rendered the 'home' crowd speechless. Healey carefully negotiated the rest of White's over, mindful of the trouble his side were in.

Donovan was now ready to deliver *his* second over. A hush descended on the LCG. His run up gathered pace and he approached the crease at top speed. He then unleashed a delivery so quickly, it was more like a red blur. It was pitched short and reared up at Farnham. All he could do was poke his bat wildly at the ball. It cannoned off the splice of the bat a looped into the air back down the pitch. Donovan quickly changed the direction of his follow through and grabbed at the ball with his outstretched right hand. He caught it!! Farnham was out caught and bowled and Elton were now, unbelievably 4 for 3!!! The Southlands players swarmed around Donovan, and their supporters danced wildly in the North Stand!

Healey and new batsman Kieron Tyler battled courageously through the next 3 overs, adding 8 more runs to their total. The Southlands bowlers were right on top the batsmen. Donovan began his fourth over just like the previous three – at rapid pace with steepling bounce. His fourth ball of the over was one too many for Tyler.

Yet again the ball rose sharply at the batsman and all he could do was fend at it. The ball brushed his left glove and whistled through to a grateful Jeff Carter behind the stumps, the 'keeper hurling the ball into the air as once again, the Southlands outfit celebrated with huge delight. It was 12 for 4 and Southlands had the game by the scruff of the neck!

Elton's overseas star Faisal Mohammad joined Healey at the crease and this really was the last chance saloon for London League side. One more wicket and the game was Southlands' surely?

Skipper Tony Fisher gave a rallying cry to his men, urging them to get just one more wicket. With Healey on just 6 and Faisal yet to score, the pressure was really on now. The Pakistan international negotiated Donovan's final 2 balls of the over and now it was Healey's turn to face White.

White was ready for Healey to attack and thought the best ploy was to bowl tidy line and length, with maybe the odd short ball mixed in. White's first two deliveries were blocked. Healey then smashed at the third, getting a thick top edge which sent the ball hurtling towards Matty at fine leg. Matty got into position to collect the ball, but somehow he let it go through his hands! The ball careered over the boundary rope for four runs. The Elton supporters cheered at a rare piece of success.

"Never mind Matty, chin up son," came the call from teammates. "You will be fine next time."

White was furious. For the next ball, he pounded in and hurled a venomous bouncer at Healey. Healey, expecting it, rocked back and played a wild hook shot, top edging the ball, unbelievably down towards Matty *again* at fine leg. The crowd sensed this was *the* moment of the match and the whole stadium took a massive intake of breath. The ball fell from the sky and into Matty's grasp. The ball popped out of his hands. He fumbled at the ball but it was too late. It had gone over the boundary for six! The crowd went wild!!

Poor Matty was devastated. Tears streamed down his cheeks as the situation dawned on him. That was surely Southlands' chance to wrap the game up. Matters went from bad to worse, as Healey, taking advantage of this huge let off, went beserk, smashing the Southlands bowlers to all parts of the LCG. From what could have been a 'game over' situation with Elton stumbling on 16 for 5, Healey and the stylish Faisal took their side to 178 for 4, before Adam Poynter trapped Faisal LBW for a beautifully crafted 53. Batsman number seven Joe Osbourne then helped Healey take their side over the 200 mark – unimaginable 2 hours earlier. Poynter then bowled Osbourne to signal another collapse. Elton stumbled from 204 for 5 to 219 all out. Healey finished unbeaten on 134, an innings which included 8 fours and an amazing NINE sixes – a National Final record. It was a phenomenal knock. All the while, Matty suffered painfully in the outfield. If only he had taken the catch . . . .

"I told you, I told you!" bellowed coach Moxon at Wimpy as the players left the field.

At tea, the Southlands dressing room, was silent as the players sat in disbelief. Had Matty taken that catch, they would probably have been chasing a total under 75. Now, although still well within reach, Healey's counter attack had mentally drained the men from Woods Hall.

7

The Final (Part 2) It Couldn't Happen Could It?

Tears once again flowed from Matty's eyes as the mood of his team mates worsened. Just then, Tony Fisher stood up and gave one of his famous fist pumping speeches. He reminded the players of the way in which they had reached this stage, and how they still had every chance of victory against the reigning champions.

"Come on lads!" He cried. "If you were offered the chance of chasing 220 before the game, to win the National, you would have took that person's hand off wouldn't you? WOULDN'T YOU??"

"Yes we would wouldn't we lads!?" replied opening bat Gary Pearce.

"Course we would!!" shouted James Hilton.

Suddenly, the mood in the room lifted and the Southlands boys were a changed team.

"Matty, forget what went on out there, get your head up and concentrate now, on us winning this thing!" urged Fisher.

The room was now a hub of noise and expectation. The top order batsmen got their batting equipment on and prepared themselves for the chase ahead. The umpires bell rang out once again, and Pearce and opening partner James Hilton took on board the messages of good luck from their colleagues and made their way out onto the LCG field.

Elton's opening bowlers Steve Fenton and Keith Blackmore loosened up and prepared themselves for their initial onslaught. Hilton and Pearce played them beautifully, carefully negotiating the early barrage. They nudged and nurdled the ball to all corners of the LCG outfield, mixed with the odd boundary, gradually building a substantial partnership. As the Elton supporters became ever quieter, they took the score over the 50 mark inside 12 overs. They serenely advanced the score to 82 before Fenton, in the first over of his second spell, had Pearce caught behind for 38, bringing Southlands' very own overseas player Shahid Zaman to the crease. The Pakistan batsman calmly took over where Pearce left off, as he and Hilton approached another 50 partnership.

Then, David Gillan was brought into the Elton attack, which paid immediate dividends. With his first ball, he immediately had Hilton back in the hutch, with another catch behind the wicket. It was 131 for 2 and with only 89 to win with 8 wickets in hand, all was set fair for a Southlands win. But Gillan had other ideas. With his fourth ball, he clean bowled Jeff Carter for a duck. Paul Vose joined Shahid with the instruction of telling Shahid to put the accelerator on. He did just that, quickly adding another 27 compared to Vose's 9. At 167 for 3, all looked rosy in the Southlands camp. Blackmore was brought back on at the Pavilion End to at least try and grab a wicket. It was a masterstroke by Rob Pickering, with Blackmore seeing off the well set Shahid for 58 and 3 balls later, Vose, clean bowled for 9. It was now 167 for 5. With 53 still needed for victory with only 5 wickets in hand, nerves began to jangle in the Southlands dressing room.

Captain Fisher was at the crease, and while he was there, the game was still Southlands for the taking. Fisher dominated the strike and skilfully added 10 more himself before Peter Stephenson was trapped LBW by Graeme Scott for a duck. With the very next ball, Kyle Donovan edged one to Aidan Healey at slip for another duck. Scott was on a hat-trick! Robbie White just about kept out the next ball, a fantastic Yorker which nearly broke White's bat! White didn't last long. In the next over, Fisher took a single off the penultimate ball, meaning White only had to see off one ball. It was one too many, as the now returned David Gillan flattened White's off stump with a gorgeous leg cutter. At 178 for 8, all looked lost for Southlands.

Adam Poynter joined Fisher and somehow, with a mixture of lusty Fisher hitting, lucky Poynter edges, crazy quick singles and nervy wides from the bowlers, the two Southlands men got their side up to 213. With only the last over to go and Fisher on strike, Southlands were the slight favourites. Gillan was to bowl the final over. He had been

Elton's best bowler by a mile. Fisher missed the first ball completely. He missed the second one to as he swung wildly at a wide one. Still 7 runs needed with now only 4 balls left. The pressure was mounting on Fisher, and the Elton supporters sensed the title was theirs for the taking now. With the third ball, Fisher again swung wildly, edging down to third man. They had to take the single. 6 required now off only 3 balls. The noise inside the LCG was deafening! Poynter was on strike. He swung and missed at the fourth ball. Both batsmen ran, but wicket keeper Joe Osbourne threw the ball and it cannoned into the stumps. Poynter was out!

On the balcony, Matty had sat watching events unfold, desperately hoping he wouldn't be required to bat. But now it was his turn to make his way into the cauldron of the LCG.

The noise levels were at maximum as he stumbled down the pavilion steps onto the field. His petrified face could be seen on the big screen in the ground as the TV cameras focussed on him as he approached the middle. With all his clothing and equipment being miles too big for him, he looked more like a mini astronaut than a cricketer! The pads were up to his stomach and the peak of the helmet almost covered his eyes! The Elton players and supporters now thought the cup was theirs. All Gillan had to do, was ensure he didn't bowl any wides or no balls, and the National Cup would be making the short journey back to Elton with him.

Matty was so nervous, he almost forgot to take his guard position, having to be reminded by the umpire at the bowler's end. Tony Fisher then had a brief word with him to try and calm him down.

"Whatever you do son, whether you hit the ball or not, just run", said Fisher.

He took middle stump guard and took a huge deep breath. He was literally shaking with fear. The Elton players took their positions, with all of their eyes fixed on Matty, like vultures eying up their prey. Gillan began his run up to deliver the second last ball of the match. Matty gulped uncontrollably as he froze on the spot. Somehow, the ball missed the off stump by a whisker, as Matty didn't even lift his bat. Fisher bellowed at Matty to run but he couldn't. His legs simply would not move. The crowd and Elton players roared with laughter at the situation. A crestfallen Fisher, having given everything, bowed his head with the realisation that the dream of winning the National for the first time in nearly 30 years was over. There was no way back now. With only one ball left and with only a six good enough to win, it was all over. Matty looked at Fisher and, realising how upset his captain was, suddenly had a huge rush of adrenalin. He was now determined to give this last ball his all.

Gillan prepared to begin his final run up. Matty took up his position at the batting crease. The crowd were frenziedly shouting 'Elton, Elton, Elton!' Fisher leant on his bat, simply waiting for the game to finish so he could get off the field.

Gillan started his run up. Matty got himself ready to face the delivery. Gillan unleashed a bouncer, safe in the knowledge Matty wouldn't get near it. The ball hurtled towards Matty's head. Matty saw it coming at him. All he could do was close his eyes and fling the bat somewhere close to where the ball was travelling. Incredibly, the ball careered off the top edge of Matty's bat. It soared high into the air, down towards deep fine leg. Aidan Healey waited for the ball to land in his huge hands. But the ball kept travelling. Healey took a step back to take the catch. The ball landed in his hands. He took another step back to control his balance – right over the boundary rope! It was a six!!

Matty, miraculously, had won the game for Southlands!!

Silence fell over the LCG. Everyone in the ground was speechless. You could almost hear a pin drop. Matty stood still, trying to come to terms with what he had done. The entire Elton team collapsed on the field in devastation. After a few seconds,
Tony Fisher ran down the pitch and picked Matty up, grabbing him tightly as the dream *was* realised. Then the rest of the Southlands team sprinted onto the field to get to their matchwinners! They chaired Matty on their shoulders and took him on a lap of honour around the LCG outfield, chanting "The New Typhoon, The New Typhoon!" Slowly, the partisan home crowd, one by one, began to cheer Matty's name.

"MATTY, MATTY, MATTY" they cried, until the whole ground came alive.

The lap of honour ended at the bottom of the pavilion steps, where the presentations took place amid a huge wall of sound. Tony Fisher received the cup and on the podium with the Southlands team, he lifted it high above his head, and the rest of the team sprayed huge waves of champagne into the air and over each other. Ticker tape filled the air to create a fantastic scene.

The added bonus for Southlands, was the fact they had now qualified for the Super League competition. This year's tournament was to be a home affair, with the Riverside Bowl hosting the event, just 10 miles from Southlands.

After the presentations were over and the crowds had left the ground, Matty sat on the outfield, just in front of the pavilion, trying to take in what had just happened. He simply could not believe he had just scored the winning runs in a National Cup final, having never scored a run for any team in his life!

"Matthew!!" cried a familiar voice.

There, at the top of the steps, stood Wimpy, and next to him, somehow, was Dad.

"Dad!! How?? How are *you* here??"

Behind Dad, a little face appeared with a massive grin on it. It was Johnny. He had telephoned Matty's house as soon as the decision was made for Matty to play. Dad had driven to the LCG as quickly as he could. The traffic around London meant he was stuck in jam after jam and arrived just in time to see the last over of the match!!

"A little dicky bird telephoned me Matthew", said Dad smiling, as he made his way down the steps.
Upon reaching Matty, father held son and as they hugged each other tightly, tears trickled gently down their faces.

The dream had come true.

The National Cup Final
Saturday September 15th, The London Cricket Ground

Elton CC

Rob Pickering	bowled White	1
Joe McShane	LBW White	0
Dan Farnham	c&b Donovan	3
Adrian Healey	not out	134 (100 balls, 8 x 4, 9 x 6)
Kieron Tyler	ct Vose bowled Donovan	2
Faisal Mohammad	LBW Poynter	53 (121 balls, 4 x 4)
Joe Osbourne	bowled Poynter	11
David Gillan	ct Fisher bowled Zaman	0
Keith Blackmore	bowled White	2
Graeme Scott	LBW White	1
Steve Fenton	bowled White	1
	Extras	11
	TOTAL all out	219
	Overs	48.4

FOW: 1-1, 2-4, 3-4, 4-12, 5-178, 6-204, 7-204, 8-206, 9-210, 10-219

Bowling: R White 5-37; K Donovan 2-40; A Poynter 2-44; P Stephenson 0-51; S Zaman 1-39.

Southlands CC

James Hilton	ct Osbourne b Gillan	54 (78 balls, 8 x 4)
Gary Pearce	ct Osbourne b Fenton	38 (50 balls 4 x 4)
Shahid Zaman	LBW Blackmore	58 (69 balls, 7 x 4)
Jeff Carter	b Gillan	0
Paul Vose	b Blackmore	9
Tony Fisher	not out	31 (64 balls 5 x 4)
Peter Stephenson	LBW b Scott	0
Kyle Donovan	ct Healey b Scott	0
Robbie White	b Gillan	0
Adam Poynter	Run out	10
Matthew Temple	not out	6 (2 balls, 1 x 6)
	Extras	14
	TOTAL for 9 wkts	220
	Overs	50

FOW: 1-82, 2-131, 3-131, 4-167, 5-167, 6-177, 7-177, 8-178, 9-214

Bowling: S Fenton 1-41; K Blackmore 2-38; D Gillan 3-52; G Scott 2-48; F Mohammad 0-31.

Southlands CC win the National Cup Final by 1 wicket

PLAYER PROFILE

Full name Matthew Temple

Nickname Matty

Age 13

Major teams Southlands CC

Batting style Right-hand bat

Club Appearances 1

Runs 6

Highest Score: 6 n.o. versus Elton CC, National Cup Final

Honours National Cup Winner.

Dream Fact Hit a 6 to win the National Cup!

Best Known For Hitting a 6 off the last ball to win the National Cup!

Do mention Winning the National Cup

Do not mention Danny Davison

SOUTHLANDS CRICKET CLUB

SOUTHLANDS CRICKET CLUB

Formed 1850

Home Ground Woods Hall

Club Honours National Cup winners 1985, 2012. County Senior League Winners 1905, 08, 1928, 1949, 1968,69, 1984. County Senior Cup Winners 1973, 75, 1983

Club Captain Tony Fisher

All time greats Trevor Temple, Bill Simpson, Jim Wakefield, Alan Moxon, Les Howell, Matthew Temple.